T0105869

Community Reconciliation Kingdom

Kent Hodge

AuthorHouse™ UK
1663 Liberty Drive
Bloomington, IN 47403 USA
www.authorhouse.co.uk
Phone: 0800.197.4150

Published by AuthorHouse 03/17/2015

ISBN: 978-1-5049-3924-9 (sc)
ISBN: 978-1-5049-3925-6 (e)

Print information available on the last page.

This book is printed on acid-free paper.

Community
Reconciliation
Kingdom

Contacts:
info@cfaithministries.org
kent.hodge@cfaithministries.org
www.cfaithministries.org

With thanks to the team in Jos. You serve God with your hearts and lives, and love his people day and night. You have literally given your lives in love.

Those who pray for and support Christian Faith Ministries: thank you for being part of the team. With thanks for everybody's encouragement.

Kent & Ruth
February, 2015

Foreword

This book is not just about "theology" but about living the way God did in this world when he put on flesh as Jesus Christ and lived among us. It has been profoundly influenced by our long term experience in Nigeria, a country which in many ways reflects the global challenges we all face.

In early 2010, surrounded by burnt-out buildings, with hundreds massacred in our area in the previous days and weeks, and rumours of terror on every side, the students at Christian Faith Institute, Bukuru, Jos, asked, "How did the early church get through persecution?" So we began to look, and that search began a journey that is turning our theology, our thinking and our living upside down.

What did the early church do? They loved their enemies, and they loved not their own lives unto death! They did this because they were not just Christians by name: they were followers of Jesus, who should do as he said and do as he did in following him. So we began not only to study what Jesus said, but also to pray that we might DO what Jesus said.

Many people were involved in deadly battles in our city: Christian and Muslim communities separated, with no communication between them. The problem was obvious. The bridges must be rebuilt. We saw such destruction, and in the middle of it all, so many youth and children with nothing to do and no hope for their future.

There were a few good stories seeping through of how Christians and Muslims stood against the tide and rescued those of “the other side”. Then some of our students found a hungry 6 year old child from a Muslim family, accidentally abandoned close by the college. They fed him, cared for him and took him to the local Mosque to be restored to his grateful people in another city. This also softened hearts.

Next, one of our team visited a Muslim friend, a man of peace and an elder in the local Muslim community at Salah, as an act of friendship. Many considered this a risky move at the time, venturing well inside “Samaria”. Then our team member invited local Muslim elders to my husband’s office, where we discussed helping their community to run a computer training centre for their youth, free of charge. They were amazed and asked, “Why are you doing this?” The answer is easy: Jesus cared for us when we were his enemies, and told us to love our neighbour the same way.

In May, 2014 our dearest friend and co-worker of more than 20 years was murdered when the vehicle he and my husband were travelling in together was ambushed by heavily armed Fulani men dressed as military. How my husband and other companions survived could only be God's hand. It deeply impacted us. This is what people face every day: the devastating loss of friend, brother, husband, and father, and the insecurity of their own lives and property. What can be done to change the lives of those who think they have no alternative but to take such desperate acts?

After the burial and in our grief the Muslim elders, who grieved together with us, took my husband and a team member to a part of Bukuru destroyed in the violence of 2009/2010, another place where Christians never go. We thought it was only persecution of Christians but when we saw the destruction done by Christians, with so many Muslim homes destroyed, women made widows and children left homeless and destitute, we knew God was calling us as Christians to change the way we live. There is a big log in our eye.

The computer training school for youth in the Muslim part of Bukuru is up and running, along with a second one in Bisichi. Relationships are growing with peace-loving, honest, industrious Muslim people who are truly friends and partners in community. Together we started a Healing Justice Fund to help people in crisis situations. The team has been able to help victims, both Muslim and Christian, of the bombing in the Jos market last December to pay their hospital bills. Help is given to widows and breadwinners to get on their feet after their loss. Families in need, unable to pay school fees or pay for surgical operations receive help. The team serves refugees and cares for destitute children: homing, feeding, schooling, clothing, and loving them, providing community.

Many of our staff and students in pastoral training come from Boko Haram ravaged areas and have suffered loss of family, friends, property and livelihood, having to bring surviving family members to a place of safety. In enduring grief together and helping our friends, we have learned that suffering and killing has occurred to both Christians and Muslims, and Christians have at times been involved in retaliation, and even pre-emption. Muslims are killed by the terrorists as often, if not more often, than Christians.

This book is a call for us as Christians to support others, caring for those who often have nowhere to turn for help. Many Christians only pray against Muslims, for their destruction, and resist Christians wanting to show love to them. Some Christians believe more in Muslim-conspiracy theories than in the teachings of Jesus. We see these responses internationally, not just in this region.

Today, many of our graduates are planting churches, preaching the gospel, and serving victims right in the midst of horrific terrorism.

Terrorists have been strongly enough armed to repel the nation's army, overrunning whole regions, creating millions of refugees including many orphaned children in acute need. The graduates' love for Jesus overflows and they follow him with joy, remaining in cities and towns under attack to serve. Many terrorists are forced into Boko Haram, so we cannot hate them. Some have been rescued by the Lord and have even enrolled in our Bible College.

Other graduates are seeing God move powerfully as people come to Christ peacefully where communities used to fight. Muslim and Christian elders have come together to learn about Jesus' kingdom and way of life and ask forgiveness of each other. One graduate said of his community who persecuted him on conversion, "I had forgiven them, but I would have nothing to do with them." That says it all: forgiveness without involvement is not really forgiveness.

A student from the Fulani people went completely blind after an attack and was in this state for about 6 months. Medical intervention achieved nothing. Students had been helping her and some grew tired. My husband told them, "When God has healed us, in our patience to serve, he will heal this lady." Last December she received a passage from the Lord, from Lamentations. She asked two staff to read the passage to her and pray for her. That night in our hostel at 2:45 AM she saw a vision of a man telling her to get up and walk, just like in the Gospels. She complained, “I am blind, so where will I walk to?” She was then instantly and totally healed. This was a community miracle. Word went out and Christians and Muslims gathered to give thanks.

Healing continues to occur between our communities and we now enjoy peace in our city. Not even Boko Haram suicide bombings (there have been several here this last year) have had the power to stir up community enmity, as our hearts change. Most people have never heard of Jesus unattached to a political or cultural agenda. We pray for revival and renewal throughout our nation as great numbers of Muslims and Christians have the intervention of the Holy Spirit and come to know the real Jesus and follow him together.

If the last 15 years of international terror and domestic conflict have proved one thing, it is that further violence is not the answer. The only answer is in living like Jesus did and taught, building community, reconciling with each other and so building His kingdom of peace on earth and goodwill towards men. That is what this book is about. God bless you as you read.

Ruth Hodge, January 30, 2015.

Community

It may be a good idea to start by saying a little about what we mean by community. For some, community might bring up thoughts of people living together in unworkable conditions. For others, it might mean domineering church life where leaders tell everybody in their "community" what to do. This idea may be conjured up by terms such as "discipleship", which for some may mean a form of legalism which easily slips in and regulates everybody's actions and beliefs. This isn't what we mean by community in this book and wrong concepts of community need to be guarded against.

Rather, what we mean by community is more to do with our motivation. We are using the term in contrast to its opposite, namely, individualism. We are using community to describe the overall aim of God's salvation: to graft us into his caring family. This is a process that begins with salvation. God's plan in transforming our lives continues as we share with one another. As we live in community, that is, as we learn to love and care for others, to make room for others and their needs in our own lives, then the nature of Christ can be formed in us. God's plan is love and this can only be shaped in us together.

This brings us to the teachings of Jesus in the four Gospels. In recent Western history, it seems, a major part of the emphasis of Jesus' teachings has been missed. We have focused on his divinity, on the way he has fulfilled prophecies of the coming messiah, about his death and resurrection and about going to heaven when we die. But when we look at the teachings of Jesus himself, we discover there is another major point we should focus on.

Jesus came at the culmination of Israel's Old Testament history. The prophets had foretold their coming judgement. Jesus came and explained the main causes for this judgement. They had largely forsaken community: people were living for their own interests, and were not caring for others. The community broke down, splintered into factions. The consequences were eventual civil war and the Roman conquest to bring order to the region. Much of Jesus' teaching was related to these symptoms.

We have largely interpreted Jesus' teachings in terms of sixteenth century Reformation ideas. When we see Jesus arguing with the Pharisees we see those arguments in terms of works versus faith. We further interpret Paul's letters in the same way. We say Jesus and Paul were against legalism as a means of salvation. Jesus, we say, was showing the futility of works to get us to heaven, and proposed faith instead. But when we look at the consistent point Jesus made in each case we find a different issue in the background. The problem Jesus had with their legalism was that the religious used it as a cloak to hide themselves from the needs of others. They weren't serving others: those of other classes, races and faiths. This was the real issue.

It is right to desert legalism for faith, but if that is where we stop we have not yet touched on the matter that Jesus addressed. He was addressing the heart of God for a caring community, across the normal barriers and divisions we erect between ourselves and others. Jesus spoke of legalism largely as a barrier to caring for others. Paul spoke of legalism largely as a barrier to unity in the church family. This was Paul's main point when speaking of our common justification by faith. Paul isn't to be read through the eyes of Western individualism, but through the community-focused eyes of God.

Jesus was not merely asking us to reject false doctrine for correct doctrine. He was not merely telling us to believe the right things. Nor is discipleship chiefly about learning the right beliefs. A disciple is one who follows Jesus, who adopts his selfless lifestyle towards those around them, drawing them into God's family by faith. Discipleship is about our relationships and how we live towards family and community. We can change to the right doctrines about faith but still be siding with the Pharisees in terms of the issue that Jesus was addressing.

Everything Jesus did in the Gospels was about care for people: visiting them, reaching across barriers of distinction and need, helping others on the Sabbath, and teaching about the Good Samaritan. It all highlighted the glaring difference between his new kingdom/caring for others' way of life and the fundamentalism of the Pharisees and their personal or nationalist kingdoms.

Reading Jesus Differently

In Western theology we are sometimes dualist. This means we separate spiritual from other issues. Jesus' teachings have often been spiritualized, and we have applied them mainly to how we go to heaven. But heaven was only a small part of what Jesus spoke about, and when he did speak about heaven it was mainly in terms of living out heaven's principles here on earth. The emphasis of Jesus was, "Your kingdom come and your will being done here on earth as it is in heaven."

This is what the Sermon on the Mount is about. In the fifth century, Augustine spiritualised the Sermon on the Mount, to line it up with the new theological shifts coming into the church. After Constantine, the Roman emperor, merged the empire with the church, the church began to rework much of its theology in line with its new methods. Augustine claimed we could fulfil Jesus' command to love our neighbour while in some instances we killed him with the sword. He said that Jesus was speaking about our spiritual attitude of heart. This was a major adjustment to what Jesus actually taught. Jesus was speaking about reconciling community, even with our enemies, here on earth.

Jesus' teachings were holistic. He didn't separate spiritual from natural. This is in keeping with the Hebrew focus of the Old Testament. Life is one. The gospel is not either spiritual or social. It is both at once. A spiritual renewal leads to social change in our lives. In Jesus there is no distinction. His interest was the kingdom coming into our hearts so there is real change in our relationships with others, which then greatly impacts on how communities are formed within our nations. His vision was of the kingdom reshaping the world, as Isaiah and the prophets foresaw. Understanding this can radically affect the way we read what Jesus said.

From the Magnificat onwards, we see this "life is one" focus especially in the Gospel of Luke. Luke consistently applies the coming of the kingdom to social change. John the Baptist presents the gospel as sharing our coats and our food with others, with being content rather than greedy. These issues were behind the malaise in Jerusalem at that time, and Jesus' way of life and his death were not just an atonement, but also the beginning of a new life and a new way of doing life. This new community would change the world in non-violence. It began in the synagogue at Nazareth. In the book of Acts, Luke shows this dynamic church in action, loving and restoring neighbours to wholeness, spiritually and economically, as the gospel and Spirit renewed their hearts.

Community Means Gathering

Sections in Luke's Gospel at first glance appear as though they are pieced together in an ad-hoc manner; however, Luke is deliberately revealing the new kingdom on earth that Isaiah prophesied, a holistic new kingdom that will renew the entire world.

We see this, for example, in the opening of Luke 11 in the Lord's Prayer, "Your kingdom come, your will be done on earth as it is in heaven." This theme connects Luke's narration in chapter 11 and what follows where, in a confrontation with the Pharisees, Jesus introduces this new kingdom and explains the stark contrast between it and the prevailing human cultural/Satanic kingdoms the Pharisees operated in all too well.

"A kingdom divided against itself shall fall." This introduces Jesus' discourse. Jerusalem would fall in that generation because of its divisions. Jerusalem then was like the vineyard in Isaiah 5, called and cleansed by God, but only to rebel and have seven stronger demons overrun and destroy the city. Their rebellion was their refusal to suffer to serve others as Jesus did. Jesus contrasts their way of doing kingdom with his renewing life and new kingdom, using two key terms: “scattering” and “gathering.”

The Pharisees scattered. Their self-centred living meant they did not care for the sick, the needy or the sinner. They were instead exclusivist, separatists, who shunned a languishing society while they themselves lived well. Society becomes divided between the “haves” and “have-nots”, between racial, gender and creedal camps, while all along the real issue was masked: protecting their wealth. In this condition of carelessness for other people, society will break down and tear apart at the seams.

A great deal of Jesus’ teaching addressed this acute first century syndrome. Jesus’ life was a direct example of an opposite kingdom: one that gathered. He gathered in the sinner, the Samaritan and the enemy of the church through forgiveness, visiting, including, healing, teaching, feeding and supporting those in need. Here was a completely liberated life that was revolutionary in that day. The liberation of Jesus, his inclusivity, non-separationist, and all-embracing lifestyle was a direct confrontation to the conservatives then, as it is to religious sentiments today.

Our human cultures are strongman orientated. One leader overcomes another and takes his goods. He divides the community between his supporters and non-supporters, helping some and depriving others. He uses any excuse to do this, even religion, or factions within religion. People build bigger barns for their own welfare, and enjoy nice comments at social events for their fine clothing, successful careers, cars, houses and children, while others in their local or global community languish. Such a kingdom must fall. More and more, people who miss out become terrorists, zealots and agitators. Civil war and infighting will tear the kingdom apart at its seams.

Here we see very clearly the nature of Jesus' kingdom and the role of the church in the world. We are gatherers, shepherds, and carers of others, whatever the creed or racial background. We refuse to treat others by a group label, but accept and gather in people to serve our whole community, to heal up the wounds and thus repair the breaches. We show God's mercy, as it has been shown to us in Christ. The gospel is demonstrated by our lives. A kingdom of mercy, that gathers, shall stand. It shall prevail in the nations. It shall fulfil the Isaianic vision. It shall cast out Satan from our community.

"He that gathers is with me." This is the face of the church, in his new kingdom.

"Separationism" is basic to Old Testament faith. In Genesis the light was separated from darkness and the land from the sea. This spoke to the Israelite of their land separated from the Gentiles. Separation was built into the Torah, between clean and unclean. When Jesus came they expected the same from him. But he showed separation means a clean heart, it means we do things God's way. We are not geographically separated from our enemies, but separate in how we respond to evil. It is our caring way of life which is to heal our enemies.

Unfolding Jesus' Shorthand

"When you give a feast, don't just invite your friends, but also the lame and sick..."

"When you greet people at the market, don't just greet your friends. Even the unbelievers do this. What difference is your faith to theirs if you only do the same as they do?"

These are shorthand ways of teaching. Jesus is not just speaking about the odd feast that we have. In Hebrew style teaching, he is using this short lesson as a starting point for us to unpack a much wider lifestyle that he is pointing to; but we could start with our special feasts, dinner parties, and Christmas celebrations.

First, our dinner parties. These are often times when we invite people we like to be with, prepare our meal in advance and tidy our home. We like these guests to make compliments on our new acquisitions and on our cooking, but what Jesus is saying is that we are to include those outside our circles. Telling us to invite them to our feasts is like telling us to, "Treat your enemies and those you do not like, those who are suffering or in need, as your own friends and family. Treat others the same way you treat your friends." Not only is this right and good and loving, but it is also the prescription for the first century predicament. Jesus said of Jerusalem, "If only you knew the things that made peace." This is one of those things.

We could even look at our Christmas feasts. We splash out on presents for our friends, maybe for those people who will give a present back to us. I remember the pressure at Christmas when I was young. If the gift I received was not as expensive as the one I gave, then I would be upset. Or, if their gift to me was more costly than my gift to them I would be embarrassed. When we consider our budget at Christmas time, how much is spent on ourselves to "stimulate our economy", while so many others languish, it is no wonder others may look on and ask, "Is this Christianity?" "Is this what the man they claim to follow did at the first Christmas in Bethlehem, when he left all to come to us, his enemies?" So this is what we could do at Christmas: what Jesus did.

Then we see what Jesus said about greeting people. We greet our friends; Jesus said we are to greet those who are outside our group. He wasn't just speaking about greeting people. This is shorthand teaching for saying that we are to treat others who are outside our group as we would treat our own people, our own family and friends, our own denomination. We are to care for others "outside" in the same way we care for ourselves. When we do not do this, society falls apart. When we do this, society is healed and stands strong. We even show this love to those who hate us and who seek our harm. This is what Jesus did and we are called to follow him as his disciples. Our world is in the shape it is today, not because of the fault of others alone, but because we in general have not yet decided to obey the simple things that Jesus showed us.

Jesus' teachings are so simple. We look for some great spiritual lesson from them, but they are just about us and our neighbour. Responding to our neighbour is godliness. This is the point in most of what Jesus taught. When we go to the temple and we remember we have wronged someone, we are to first go to that person and rectify what we have done, before we worship. That is, treating our neighbour the right way, no matter who that neighbour is, is worship. We do not come to God in worship by our self, but only and always with our neighbour, by how we treat and reconcile with others, including our enemies. All Jesus' teachings are community teachings, because community that heals and blesses individuals is the heart of God. God reached out to his enemies to build a new community, so if we do that to others, then we are his children.

This is where we come to Jesus' idea of faith. He said that if we do not do these things then how is our faith different to the pagans? He said faith is not just something we hold to in our hearts, or in a creed, or in formal worship, or in the group that we identify with. It is not saying the "sinner's prayer." It is a way of life: his way of life. It is discipleship; being his follower. This is faith.

"When you give a gift do not give to those who will return the gift, but to those who cannot return the gift."

This is so against our normal social sentiments. If someone invites us for dinner, we think it is polite to bring something. Not that they need it, but if we do not, people may reject us. We give to ourselves, to those from whom we expect a return. We see this also in ministry relationships. This just shows, on a small scale, part of what contributes to the big problems that we face in the world today; yet we like to put these problems down to other people. While the faults of others play a part, we start with our lives, with what Jesus told us to do. Jesus' message was not essentially about the Romans, or zealots and terrorists; it was about us, the people of God, what we should do, because we have the light and the solution, if we will apply it.

The world is healed as we give freely to those who have need, not to ourselves. These shorthand teachings of Jesus are our remedy for community breakdown, showing how his new kingdom comes amongst us, which Jesus gave to us in plain, simple language.

We need to be on the road to community, which just means including others in our lives and resources. It may not be an easy way of life at first. Including others is often hard; we are not used to it. They are usually difficult people. Certainly they are always different to us. Difference is always a challenge. We also see their faults more than we see our own faults, but the thing is, the gospel is all about love and love is learning to adjust ourselves to other people, to receive and to help them, and to allow ourselves to be helped by them. Jesus comes into our lives with his friends. It is a package. We cannot go with him without going with his community. We grow in Jesus when we grow together with everyone else.

A Surprising Gospel and Lord

In the first century many people in Israel were expecting a messiah of vengeance to come. He would punish their enemies and restore Israel to their glory, as it was in David's time. He would be a messiah like David, who would make their enemies suffer. At the very least he would stop their enemies from hurting them.

This is our usual religious expectation; the way we see God. In all human religion we see God as the one who comes to bless us, increase us, provide us with health, prosperity and wellbeing, and to deal with our enemies. But this is not the God that Jesus showed us when he came. Yes, he heals us, but it is his life and community life that he wants us to see, to follow and to have. This is healing. This is being like him.

The teaching of Jesus was an absolute scandal in his time. It was opposite to all expectations. He critiqued his own people and nation, not the enemy. He said it was a blessing to suffer, not to do well in human terms. It is funny when someone says, "God bless you." When we look through everything in the Gospels that Jesus called a blessing, we notice that he does not mean what we mean by the term at all. His teaching was simply treason in the eyes of his people.

Our human perception of God is one of the most dangerous things on earth. It is because everyone sees God as being on their side, as the one to bless them and to punish their enemies that we cannot appreciate the community kingdom that Jesus spoke of. We cannot come to his kingdom fulfilment here on earth while this is our vision of who God is. Our perception of God leads us to division, segregation, prejudice, lack of support for others, and war. Jesus did not come to enhance this type of faith in our lives.

Religion can intensify guilt, or "the knowledge of good and evil" in our conscience. The guilt of Adam's self-centred response to God's good love struck him, enslaved him and drove him from God's presence to hide. God did not drive Adam from his presence and God's love did not change towards Adam, he only protected Adam from living eternally in that Satan-bound state.

This guilt was Satan's plan to enslave man, as outlined in Romans 7. It is also Satan's plan to use religion to enhance our hostility towards each other. It produces all kinds of violence, as we try to free ourselves from guilt by transferring it onto others. The Pharisees did this and Saul of Tarsus was led by this, all the while thinking he was doing the will of God. This manifests in broken relationships, church splits, and in more serious ways. It is the nature of propaganda, which constantly surfaces whenever we have a problem. God's reconciliation in Christ restores our conscience, enabling us to love, rather than to prosecute, the ungodly.

Jesus could not be understood as a messiah. He was a threat to nationhood and to personal interest. He would not uphold the norms of our divided society. This type of messiah would just have to go. He would have to be put to death. I imagine Jesus would get the same reception if he came today. The sword he brought was against himself and his followers. What did Jesus say should be our response? He said our response should be to love our enemies, promote peace, serve their needs, and if need be die for the gospel. Jesus came to show us an entirely different type of God: the true Father.

Kingdom Leadership

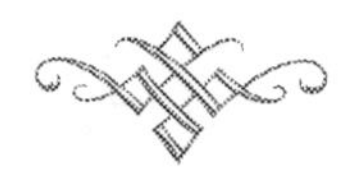

Jesus never lifted a finger against the enemies of God's people. He refused to call down fire on the villagers who rejected him, healed the ear of one of those arresting him, allowed Barabbas the insurgent to go free and forgave those who crucified him. We have a problem today and in a way it is a good problem: God does not only love us, but he also loves our enemies and desires that they come to repentance. If God was not like this, we would not benefit from his good nature either. So we need to remember this when others harm us, and love them. They need grace for change too.

This is what the Sermon on the Mount is about. "The messiah will deliver us from Rome", they thought. But Jesus said, "You are blessed when you are persecuted." Is that what we go to church to hear on Sunday? This messiah simply was not doing his job. This was an offence.

"If anyone calls you to carry their load one mile, carry it two miles." This was a reference to the Roman law, that whenever a Roman solider needed help on his journey he could order anyone on the road to assist. That person was then obliged by Roman law to help carry the soldier's load for one mile. For the Jew, this law was blasphemy. "What, are we to help the desecraters of the temple, idolaters, and child killers, those who enact ungodly laws in our society?"

The Roman soldiers were brutal. They were among the main abusers and terrorisers of humanity of that day. Surely the messiah would come and do justice against them. We have a very keen sense of justice, especially our justice, especially when it comes to our suffering. But Jesus sees justice differently to us. This is the scandal of his message. "Carry his load two miles", Jesus said. "What, are we to help a soldier carry his weapons to the next village, only to terrorise our family members who live there?" Yes.

"If someone sues you for your coat, allow them to have your shirt also." "Give to everyone who asks, and do not lend." "Love your enemies." "Do good to do those who persecute you. Bless them." "Do not (violently) resist evil."

Wow, what are we going to do with all this? Love in the Hebrew sense is not just an attitude of the heart. It means to take care of the needs of others. It is something we do. We cannot agree with Augustine who said that Jesus did not mean what he said here, but was only speaking of a heart forgiveness towards our enemies. Jesus meant it, and showed what he meant by his own life. He clearly told us, "Take up your cross and follow me". There is not another kind of Christianity than this.

Why don't we agree with this?

1. Maybe it is because of our materialism. We have become used to materialistic views in our modern way of life, and we often take them for granted. "It is right to protect private property." This is a major tenant of our societies today. But Jesus said, "Beware of covetousness, because a person's life does not consist of his property." Yet we will sue for property today, for divorce settlements, for our share of an estate when someone we love dies, and for every other thing. How can this be reconciled with the life Jesus lived?

2. Maybe it's because we believe that ultimately it is "eye for eye" justice that will safeguard our societies. "We are doing this to uphold law and order in our land." Why didn't Jesus do it then? Why did he rescind "eye for eye and tooth for tooth?" Why did he say, "Just forgive as your heavenly Father forgives."? Why did his teaching on forgiveness appear so radical and so shock the sentiments of the disciples? Why did he rescind punitive justice, in favour of restorative

> justice? Because punitive justice does not work in the end, and restorative justice is God's way and heart. God came in Christ to show us who he is.

Restorative justice is reconciliatory. Jesus is speaking here about reconciliation. "There is something more important than your goods and even your lives on this earth, and that is reconciliation, and that is why I gladly lay down my life for reconciliation and fellowship between God and man. Follow me." Jesus is showing us how to reconcile with our enemies his way. There is something more important than individualism and that is fellowship with our enemies. They are people: love them more than we love our own lives. That is what God did.

This is the highest issue in our lives. God's whole kingdom is about reconciliation. This is what it means to be salt and light. It means to love our enemies while suffering at their hand. "Father forgive them, for they do not know what they are doing." When they have hurt us, then we give to them and help them. This is preaching the gospel. Preaching is a calling to Jesus' lordship, which is faith lived out his way.

"Consider the lilies and the birds. They do not build barns, yet God feeds them. Aren't you so much more loved by God than them?"

This was said in the context of us following Jesus and doing what he said. Obeying. God will care for us. We do not have to live the way our society says that we should. We do not need to take hold of our own lives. We do not have to hold our investments for our future, thinking of ourselves; we can care for others who have no future. We can love our enemies, and God does and will love us with an overwhelming abundance. It may not always be comfortable for us, but there will always be an abundance of love, fellowship and real life.

"Do not fear little flock, for it is your Father's great pleasure to give you the kingdom."

God is waiting for the world to learn and for us, his people, to show and lead the way, by his wonderful and special grace. When we consider the truth as Jesus showed us, we realise how longsuffering God is with his creation; how long he waits for us. His nature and ways are so very different to what we have thought. The fall of man is so engrained within us and within all our cultures.

The Sermon on the Mount is Jesus' community teaching. This is how we live when we want to follow Jesus in building community and bring about his kingdom on earth as it is in heaven. This is the way. This is the way that is opposite to darkness. God will not overcome evil using its methods. He will stick by his own methods and nature, which he has shown to us in Jesus. God remains God no matter what the enemy does, and overcomes only through good. This is what makes his way "hard" in the world's eyes. This is what requires patience and produces in us his characteristics, his nature, transforming us into his true image.

When we say we are "followers of the way", we do not just mean a way of going to heaven, but a way of life on earth: Jesus' way of life. We have often said Jesus suffered for us as redeemer, and suffering is now finished, and therefore we do not follow his way of life: it was just for him as redeemer. But that is not what Jesus said. As for Christ, so for his body. We are one in suffering, in model, in leadership and in life and we are sharers in his full kingdom.

Suffering is a very interesting subject and our view of it is often very ungodly. Take Isaiah 53 for example, which clearly portrays the sufferings of Christ. The people "esteemed him smitten, stricken by God." They despised his suffering. We are followers of this Christ when we see him in the suffering of others and take those people to our heart. Isaiah 53 is a direct challenge to us in our position in relation to a suffering world. If we stand away from it, we stand away from Christ.

Victory over Our Enemies

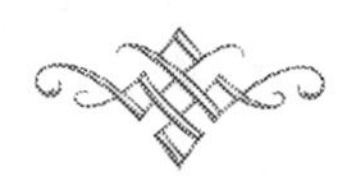

Where do we start with this? The Old Testament is full of violence. Violence has become human culture since the fall. God worked with in that context, while giving his people a witness of the new kingdom that was coming, when he would appear in his Son, show us his way and give us a new heart.

The Old Testament is full of images and cultural symbols of that time and these were employed to speak of God's coming kingdom; but the way in which these images and symbols would be fulfilled was hidden and remained a mystery due to our own hard (lit': fat, self-centred) hearts. If there is one thing that history shows it is our utter inability to predict how God will fulfil his kingdom prophecies; yet we remain self-confident in our predictions, sometimes even putting them before our fellowship with those who hold other views.

"You shall break them with a rod of iron, you shall crush them to pieces like a potter's vessel." Psalm 2:9

We could call up verse after violent verse like this in the Old Testament. God promised clearly that he would subdue Israel's enemies. He said he would do so with absolute decisiveness. These promises are couched in complex and brilliant prophetic poetry, but they boil down to two things: 1. God would subdue all our enemies. 2. He would do this with a complete and total victory. The subjugation would be absolute, final and eternal. Let's add a third one: 3. This would impact and renew the whole of God's created order, including the whole of the earth.

Daniel homed in on this apocalyptic vision of the coming kingdom. In chapter two we see a statue representing human empires of oppression. A stone from heaven comes and smites and crushes the statue to dust, which is then blown away. The stone then fills and renews the whole world. Many in Israel were ready and waiting for this kind of messiah to come and crush their enemies. Daniel even gave the date and place: first century Palestine.

What shocked Israel was that because they were part of Adam's fall, as Romans 7 explains, they too were part of this statue. They too were an enemy of God. Oh dear! This is getting a bit complex: "It's not what enters the stomach that defiles a man, but what comes out of the heart. This defiles a man." Jesus said they too may share in Gehenna, the place for "Gog and Magog", a symbol which designates God's enemies. "Look, we don't want to hear this, Jesus. Just do the job we expected."

Then Jesus gave parables about this kingdom and how it would come. In the parable of the sower, no matter which type of bad soil it was, the issue in each case was selfishness. They just did not want to serve their enemies. This kingdom is shaping up to be something quite different than they had thought. In the parable of the mustard seed that follows, the birds, which symbolised enemies (in their culture birds were often the symbol used for enemies and these birds were the enemies which took away the seed in the first parable), now come and take rest under the branches of the church. That is, in his kingdom, his people care for their enemies. Another monumental twist and outrage!

The big shock, which we still often fail to grasp in our own time, is that God would achieve his great victory, not by destroying our enemies, but by our joint reconciliation. He would break down the barrier between us (in our old hearts) and bring us together into a new creation. When he tears down the statue, he tears down the enmity in our hearts. This *enmity* is the enemy, not flesh and blood. On the cross, Jesus destroyed the enmity between us and God, and the new nature he gives us works to destroy the enmity between us and others. This puts us on the same path of reconciliation and peacemaking as followers of him: "Blessed are the peacemakers, for these shall be called the children of God."

It's this new type of kingdom, community, reconciliation, that comes to reign within our hearts, which tears down the oppressive powers in our own natures and nations, and rebuilds us in Christ's likeness. This is Daniel's vision, brought to life in the gospel. This is the gospel: the way God saves and renews the world, which is his plan, not just to save us as individuals.

The great twist in the gospel is that God comes in Christ and takes the crushing of the law himself, to ransom us from the true enemy, from Satan's camp. He becomes crushed as powder, through the joint violence we and our enemies did to him. He takes our sin by our crushing of him. He identifies with us all and becomes that statue in Daniel which is crushed, and this is how he crushes our enmity. God allows himself to be crushed in Christ, by our oppression, sin and violence, so he can then forgive it and break its power (Isaiah 53:10). The "crushing" is transformed by Christ into a gospel symbol of self-giving reconciliation, which we are to emulate as his followers (Rev 2:26-27).

So we see again so plainly, we are not to be the accusers of our enemy, of the sinner, like the Pharisees accused the woman caught in adultery, but we are to be their servants, just as Christ served us. We are the ones who place ourselves between the sinner and the accuser and help them, to lead them to grace and redemption. This is the atonement, by which God in Christ made peace in our conscience and made us messengers of peace with others. We are to love, heal, forgive, care for, serve and draw our enemy, as God has done to us.

The rod of iron (Psalm 2) symbolises a complete victory. He has subdued our enemies through reconciliation. As Paul said, "He made both Jew and Gentiles (Israel's enemies) one through the cross, breaking down thc middle wall of separation." What an indignity in Paul's day! "A leader of the Pharisees, gone over to the enemy like this, bringing us together as one. Paul too must go."

The wonderful part of the messianic prophecy in Psalm 2 is that in Hebrew culture, when the potter's vcssels were broken and crushed to powder, the powder was made into very strong cement, which was then used to hold the stones together in their new houses. Jesus became this crushed powder and through his Spirit, his cross-shaped love is the *adhesive* by which enemies with different traditions are reconciled, joined and built into a new house in the Lord.

Because of his love, God's crushing of his enemies is taken by himself in Christ and by this he redeems, destroys Israel's enmity with her foes, reconciles us together in one body and builds a new creation of peace. By this he claims total victory over Satan in a way that only the true God could do. He did this without a single concession to Satan's methods. In doing this he builds a new indestructible community and renews the world. What can we say to this? We don't have enough praise to respond appropriately to it. He calls us to follow in these same steps that he made.

We need to take care in how we interpret scripture, before we follow our untransformed instincts. First ask, what is God like, what has he shown us in Jesus? Jesus, in the Gospels, is how we interpret the rest of scripture, because if we have seen him, we have seen the Father. God is calling us to serve our enemies, not to call for their destruction. This is his plan of renewal. When we seek to destroy them, or even ignore and not help them, we become like them instead of becoming like God. We are to follow his way, as seen in Christ.

The Biggest Surprise of All

It is all part of the same big shock: that God would act to defeat our enemies by reconciling them to himself and then call us to walk in that reconciliation, even towards our own enemies. This view of God changes everything about the way we live our lives and treat other people, especially those who disagree with us.

The biggest surprise of all in our whole recorded history is to finally find out what God is really like, what all our religions have not revealed, about his true nature. The biggest surprise of all is to find out how this great omnipotent God does battle against his enemies. Isaiah says God looked and there was no man to help, therefore his own arm brought salvation. He would dress as a man of war and go into battle with a tunic of righteousness and a belt of truth. He was coming to Israel to do battle against our foes.

This is what the apocalypse refers to. Literally, it means to unveil, to reveal. What is being revealed? The surprise! The way God does battle. The way he would fulfil his promises. The way he would take back sovereignty over a fallen world and pour out his blessings upon all nations and renew our entire land. This is not the individualist gospel we have become used to in recent times. This is a community gospel, through which God will advance his global renovation.

In Isaiah 45, God declares his word against all the idolatry of the world. He declares his decree against all kings of the earth. God would come and rule the nations. He would utterly conquer and rout out every enemy of the land. He would take back sovereignty over all the kingdoms. "As I live declares the Lord, to me every knee shall bow and every tongue confess." But the biggest surprise of all is how God would fight, how he would go into battle against these kings and nations and accomplish once again his sovereign rule over human lives, cultures and governments.

Imagine Saul of Tarsus and the shock this was to him. He was busy making the world a better place, stoning those (women) caught in adultery and blasphemers, killing Christians, fighting the enemies of unrighteousness and ungodliness, implementing God's good law, and then suddenly his whole mind is turned inside out. This would have been so hard to bear. Jesus appeared to Saul and said this is not the way he does things, and showed Saul instead all he would suffer for his kingdom.

What a journey Paul travelled before he could sing this poem in Philippians 2: *the great apocalypse*. God the Word, could become a baby without a room, be accused of being a bastard, be a refugee in Egypt, a low carpenter in Nazareth, carry a towel as a house servant to wash our feet, be condemned by injustice, and through his own death as a slave on a Roman Empire cross conquer his enemies. God would fight, not by killing his enemies, but by dying for them and serving them. This is completely unimaginable to our human thinking. It is contrary to all our cultural myths about warfare and Superman. It is only in Jesus and the Gospels we can see this. Such humility from one so far above us, in contrast to our human cultures, is the biggest shock of all.

This is why the book of Revelation is so named. It unveils how God's promised reign on earth comes about. It begins with the cross and unfolds through his church, which takes on the same inner spirit. John hears a voice saying, "The lion of the tribe of Judah has prevailed", and he turns and sees a lamb that was slain. So the lion is really a lamb? This is the apocalypse: the Lamb of God. God comes as a lamb to defeat his enemies.

It is a mistake to look at Jesus in his glorification and think his character or mode of leadership has changed. We think this in order to invent a political "Jesus" to deal with our enemies. As a friend said, "It is the slain lamb who rules the world and this is good news for the little people." Or was it Mary who said that? It's the essence of Jesus' message.

The lamb is the main image in Revelation, referred to 29 times. There are images of Christ at war, but these show God's "weakness" is his strength and victory. He is mighty in battle, but with truth, righteousness, mercy and love. He treads out the winepress of God's wrath, but as depicted in church art he does this by his own death "outside the city", thus conquering his enemy death and reviving the nations (Isaiah 25-27, 63, Gen 49:11). He took the cup and identified with our Armageddon, by the hand of the same two beasts of Revelation: Jerusalem and Rome. Everything Jesus said about the destruction of the temple he also bore as the temple of God. He has a sword going out of his mouth, by which he slays his enemies, but this indicates the gospel Word which goes out to the nations, reconciling the world. This is how God fights.

Revelation depicts God's vengeance and judgment, but his judgement is not unfolded by God's violence, but by man's violence coming back on himself. Those who slay the lamb and his martyrs become drunk in their blood. They are handed over to their own ways, lose all sense and head for self-destruction. God allows the wicked to destroy each other. The way of the wicked is self-destructive. So it was throughout the Old Testament prophets and in AD 70, the destruction of Jerusalem, and so it will always be with the enemies of God: those who do not repent from violence destroy themselves. And God takes no delight in it.

The symbols of war depict a moral and legal encounter. God only engages and overthrows Satan through Christ and his cross. In Genesis 1 we see the nature of this warfare. It is choice, depicted by light and darkness. "I put before you life and death, choose life." In other ancient creation narratives the gods did actual battle, which suited the violence of the societies. But God is omnipotent and there is no hand to hand combat with him. He overcomes evil with good.

Christ the Lamb is God's apocalypse and wisdom and way: the way of victory over his and our enemies, and over the enmity in our own hearts. The enemy to defeat is within us. We fight with weapons of self-giving, service, peace and reconciliation.

A Reconciling Church

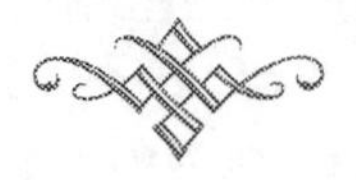

The reconciling action of God in Christ continues in and through the church. Paul's identification with Christ's reconciling servant/sufferings is throughout his letters, not because Paul lived in tough times, but because this is how God's kingdom comes and spreads in the nations. The astonishing action of Christ in his reconciling self-giving is to fill every action of the church in the world.

We see here two things:

1. The posture of the church. We are not lords, but servants to draw and renew hearts, lives and cultures the same way Christ did on the cross. We are kings and priests to God, but to the world we are servants, ambassadors of a heavenly kingdom, pointing to genuine community, reconciling, serving life. This was God's posture in Christ and it is our posture. This is how God's kingdom comes and reigns in the world, unlike other kingdoms which force, manipulate and coerce their way through worldly means.

2. It is God's purpose to reconcile all things under his entire creation into Christ, not to destroy them. This is the leavening of Christ's kingdom, until "all things are made new."

"That in the fullness of time he might gather together in one all things in Christ." Ephesians 1:10

The fullness of time means the gospel age. In the fullness of time Christ appeared in the flesh to begin this kingdom, and in the church age gather into it all things, and this will continue until all things are gathered and renewed. The "all things" that are gathered includes everything in heaven and in earth, meaning populations, cultures, governments, faiths.

This "all things" theme occurs throughout the New Testament, and indicates the progressive bringing under the feet of Christ all enemies. But the surprise again is the way this is done: not through violent force and conquest, not through a domineering, "colonialization" attitude, but through the reconciling action of the Spirit in the Christlike lives of his followers.

We could say that this reconciling occurs in respect to two things: 1. To people of different races, cultures, traditions, genders, and classes within the church. 2. Between the church and the world; how we reach and transform our enemies. Remember, this was the Old Testament problem: what were we to do about our enemies, who keep rising up and troubling us, however often we defeat them? Christ showed us God's way.

First, reconciliation within the church:

The reconciling process is the means by which our lives are renewed and brought together in one caring family to Christ's benevolent reign. We come with our differences and are conformed to Christ's image of love, not to the image of any one human culture. God is a God of immense and rich diversity, which is to be fully celebrated in love, liberty and appreciation.

In chapter two of Ephesians we see this reconciling process between Jewish and Gentile believers. They are brought into one body, with their cultural distinctions: because being justified by faith alone, these different traditions are brought into God's kingdom and transformed to reflect Christ's love. Again, there was no greater liberating, inclusive and embracing dynamic in the Roman world than the gospel. It was an utter surprise. It is something that even today we hardly embrace, even among Christians of different backgrounds.

Let us digress a little here. I think this is important when looking at our posture as the church. I agree with a statement I once heard: "If the Reformation had focused more on Ephesians than on Romans and Galatians, the last 500 years may have been somewhat different." This person wasn't referring to a problem with Romans or Galatians, but ways in which these letters have sometimes been understood and applied. If Ephesians had been the focus, the theme of reconciliation in Ephesians may have been more apparent to us, and resulted in less separatist and Pharisaic actions in our dealings with each other and with our world.

It is very common to hear, "If any man preach any other gospel, let him be accursed", as we divide further and separate from other believers: as though this was some kind of holy virtue. I suggest that this way of taking this verse in Galatians is the opposite of what Paul intended. Paul was correcting Peter for this very type of Pharisaic spirit. Peter had withdrawn from some believers because their customs were different. He had taken the liberty out of the gospel, and rebuilt the wall of division Christ had torn down by his blood. This made Paul boil.

Paul's purpose in Romans and Galatians was not to condemn Jewish practices, but to show that since justification is by faith, we can receive each other whatever our cultural or religious practices may be. Paul's point about justification by faith is to draw us together in one body, to love each other at one table of fellowship, though one eats meat and another does not. He was not against circumcision, but against insistence on circumcision for fellowship. Paul's point in all these epistles is community in diversity (love), not division; not taking a stand and then dividing again. The stand we take is the stand of fellowship, though others put pressure on us to divide.

One unfortunate outcome in the way that we have wrongly taken Paul is that in church history we have often condemned the Jews and persecuted them because of their traditions. Imagine that, the church called to serve and to suffer, becomes the persecutor of others. This has sadly often been the posture of the church up to our present day. Instead, we should be accommodating the Jews' traditions and drawing them to reconciliation through the love of Christ. This was the view of the apostles (Acts 15:20-21).

In the last 500 years, this same fury has been directed at the Roman Catholics and their traditions by the Protestants. There are always errors to correct in all of our lives, but these errors are to be corrected with and through a reconciling spirit. This is the only way we can listen to and understand others properly, rather than holding an arrogant "know all" position. This reconciling spirit is the nature of the church. I would suggest that if we are not showing this nature then we are not living as his church.

How can we partake of the Lord's Supper whilst remaining divided? This is what Paul means by "not discerning the Lord's body", and we so often fail to discern his body in other believers. God's family is his body. Paul was saying, if we do not discern his body in other believers, or in the poor, then we eat and drink wrongly. The Lord's Supper is not an individual, private thing, as we have often taken it to be, but a supper: communion, community, meal together, laying down our lives for his whole body and serving our community.

This is a serious matter: One, because our separation pulls down the cross of Christ, by which he tore down the wall of division between us. Two, how can we take the next step, and be a reconciling, drawing and renewing force in the world, when we cannot do it in our own house?

We are to be those who "commit acts of reconciliation" with all those who call on the name of our Lord Jesus Christ. These are deliberate actions we take towards believers outside our normal circles of fellowship, more than just a change in our attitude. It is amazing that when people reach out in reconciliation with other sectors of the church, they are often labelled as heretics. This is exactly what Jesus suffered, because he crossed lines. "The Son of man has nowhere to lay his head." His interest was his Father's will, not our camps.

Second, the church serving and reconciling in the world:

Ephesians explains this process.

"God's intention for the church is that God would use it to show his abundant wisdom to the world's principalities and powers in high places." Ephesians 3:10

Principalities refer to the powers that control or influence human behaviour. These may be spiritual powers that coerce, or powers on earth, such as governments, faiths, cultures and economic powers. These entities link up and control the nations and world.

Remember again, back in the Old Testament, God said he would take dominion over all these powers and, by doing so, restore the world. When we come to Jesus in the Gospels, and to Paul in his letters, we see how God is planning to do this. Christ's wisdom is not coercion, or to force in a worldly sense, but "the foolishness of God" is service. Now we continue this service through the church. It is through this foolishness of God, "which is wiser than men", that God plans to bring to nothing these worldly powers: that is, overcome and remove their satanic basis and reconcile them into his kingdom, to bless the nations.

Remember our posture. When it comes to the church transforming government, we are not the government's chaplain, wielding its power over the lives of others, taking advantage for our group and vision, while consenting to government's wrong doing. We are witnesses to government with our lives, as Jesus demonstrated for his church before Pilate. Jesus was not a "king maker", but a prophet to kings. The church follows Jesus. Only a witness divested of self-interest transforms both ourselves and our governments.

Many in Jesus' day were expecting the messiah to come and fix things by taking power. This is also seen in Satan's temptation of Jesus, to fulfil his Isaianic mission through the governments of this world. Instead Jesus chose his cross, and called us to do the same. Having influence in the governments of this world won't secure the church. It's another surprise of God's "upside-down" ways seen in Christ. Nothing in history has influenced leadership more than the cross of Christ, the "foolishness of God". Taking up our cross is the way of the church. Serving secures the church's message and shines the light on our nations.

Our witness is for the Word and the action of Christ, against self-seeking interests, and for the common good of all people. Our witness is for building reconciling community at home and abroad, for peace among all groups, in demonstration of the love of Christ who gave himself for the whole world, not just for us.

As for economic powers and cultures, our witness to them is the church's caring community, rather than commercial materialism; caring for each other within the church and reaching out with the same care to a suffering world, rather than self-indulgence.

As for other faiths, our witness to them is sharing with them the same loving community in outreach, "not just thinking of our own welfare, but also of the welfare and need of others"; while learning from them in the common grace we share, and being a witness to them of Christ through his Word, grace and love. This is not an oppositional and arrogant posture, but a posture that reflects the life of Christ to outsiders, as seen in the Gospels.

Even though many of the leaders involved in first century Judaism tried to stamp out the gospel and church and were involved in the killings and persecution of many Christians, still the believers continued to meet in the synagogues. The synagogues were largely Christ deniers, yet the Christians on the whole did not hold an oppositional stance towards them. The evidence suggests the Christian community acted in love towards the rest of their Jewish community and even continued in worship with them.

Since that time greater levels of disrespect developed and spoiled our interaction with the Jewish community. This same style has also impacted our interaction with the Islamic community and other faith based communities. The gospel and its values need to be witnessed to constantly and with clarity but also with respect, in the context of our involvement in the lives of others, our honouring of their culture, in serving and self-giving and forgiving when harmed.

We earnestly desire the promise of God to continue, for the rivers of water to flow from his church, bringing the Word of life by the Holy Spirit's guidance and power to all communities and people, and transforming the nations by the fruit we bear.

In summary, the powers God is bringing to nought include those in our own character, and our own behaviour. This is where the powers are seated and work from. Paul lists these powers in Corinthians: a divided party spirit, disunity, immorality, greed in taking others to court rather than suffer wrong, neglecting the poor, showing spiritual superiority, not accommodating the traditions and views of others: anything against the kingdom of love.

All these are self-centred, community-destroying powers. When communities are destroyed, then individuals suffer. God, through his new reign in our hearts, is opposed to this suffering. God does not overcome these powers violently, but through our renewed hearts. If God overcame with violence and not with mercy we also would be destroyed. These are the powers God is bringing down through his church, as he renews our own lives within the church towards each other, and then sends the church as a new body to be witnesses into the world. God is implanting us with his reconciling powers of the fruit of the Spirit.

This is God's purpose in Christ, who is head of the body: to reconcile and then renew the whole of his creation. The entire gospel is reconciliatory in its purpose, in its destiny, its spirit, and in its program. God overcomes and subdues his enemies through reconciliation, and he uses the self-giving lives of his people to do so, just as he showed us in Christ, who gave himself for us. If there is one word to describe the gospel it is reconciliation: which is to build our nations through Christ's world-changing community, fulfilling God's promise to Abraham.

"For in him all things were created: things in heaven and on earth, visible and invisible, whether thrones or powers or rulers or authorities; all things have been created through him and for him. He is before all things, and in him all things hold together. And he is the head of the body, the church; he is the beginning and the firstborn from among the dead, so that in everything he might have the supremacy. For God was pleased to have all his fullness dwell in him, and through him to reconcile to himself all things, whether things on earth or things in heaven, by making peace through his blood, shed on the cross." Colossians 1:16-20

"God's fullness shall fill all things", until "the knowledge of the glory of the Lord shall cover the earth, as the waters cover the sea."

The scripture is not only historical narrative; to the Jews it was also redemptive promise. When Israel came out of Egypt they saw the creation story repeated in their lives. God brought a new nation out of disorder, gave them a good land and made them his priesthood, to reflect his image to the nations in service. They were God's new Adam in the world. This redemptive purpose, to bless the nations, the whole land/world, was not abandoned by God when Adam or Israel fell, but is fulfilled through Christ in his church. "But you are a chosen people, a royal priesthood, a holy nation, God's special possession, that you may declare the praises of him who called you *out of darkness into his wonderful light*." This is the creation narrative fulfilled in a serving church.

Justification has been so central to Western theology that its purpose has sometimes slipped from our view: that the image of God seen in Christ should be reflected by God's family into the world to set creation free from its bondage. The whole earth becomes God's good Promised Land.

What is God Really Like?

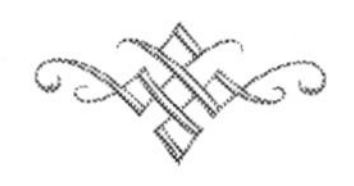

Our view of Jesus as seen in the Gospel accounts may be challenged by other parts of the scripture. We know that in Christ we clearly see the real nature of God. That is God's intention, to send Christ so that we might truly know him and become like him. This is the only way our relationships and world can be healed.

But in other parts of scripture, as well as in some of our doctrines, God can appear violent.

When we are confused about who God is, and what he is like, it affects our lives as Christians. Our image of God is important, because we are transformed into the image we have as we worship and we reflect that image in the world. This is why it is the image of God in Jesus Christ that is most important. If we take up some other image, or a confused picture of God, we can become distorted in our lives and violent in our societies.

This has frequently occurred throughout history. The church has often adopted the wrong posture towards its enemies. We have justified it from scripture passages we have taken wrongly and doctrines that have not truly reflected God's nature as seen in Christ.

We are faced with choices today on the nature that we reflect, and must make the correct biblical decisions as disciples of Jesus. This is important for us, so let us have a brief look at a few ideas that may give a skewed picture of God's nature.

1. *God's kingdom comes through war and destruction*

This may be taken from passages like Matthew 24, where Jesus mentions "wars and rumours of wars", or from 2nd Peter, where Peter speaks of the world being destroyed by fire. We look at these in my book called *Rediscovering Revelation*, so I won't repeat those points here. In Western culture we often misinterpret these passages using Greek cultural principles, not Hebrew ones.

The main comment to make here is that this is how many Jews thought the kingdom would come in the first century. They presumed it would come by God destroying their enemies. Jesus very clearly denounced that view.

I was in a church once (and this has happened on countless occasions) and a brother said to me, "God is using America to destroy the Arab nations in the last days...", and he went on. I was told you had to go to a mosque to hear such propagation of violence! Apparently you can hear it in churches as well.

2. God is a wrathful judge

The idea here is that, since God is a God of wrath, then our wrath can also be justified. How many times do we hear about our licence to have "righteous anger", as though we were capable of such a thing? We are not fit for this, which is why scripture says, "Vengeance is mine, says the Lord."

But God's wrath does not show him to be violent. The main place in scripture where God's wrath is described is in Romans 1. There the words used repeatedly are "handed over", "given over". God's wrath consists of removing the protective hedge around man, and allowing him to go his own way. Wrath is taking away his transforming conviction. We are the ones who do this, when we refuse correction. When that happens, man brings upon himself the consequences of his own actions. God does not do violence against man.

3. God sent fire on Sodom

The book of Job gives us insight into this. Here, Satan appears before God, accusing him on

Job's account. God then removes the hedge and allows Job to be tested. Satan goes out from the presence of the Lord and sends affliction on Job though war, weather and fire. It is said that, "fire from God in heaven came down", when the fire was not from God. This is the way the Hebrew expressed calamity in the Old Testament, due to their correct belief in the sovereignty of God.

We see the same expressions being used with regard to Sodom and the Flood. God's judgement consisted of removing his hedge and allowing mankind to reap the consequences of their own actions. The consequences of man's fall impact on our natural environment. God's part was to be patient, to show mercy and then, after judgment, to rebuild and renew the land. But God had no part in the violence that brought man's destruction.

4. *God killed the firstborn in Egypt*

Actually he did not: it was the "angel of the Lord" and this is a similar phrase to the one in Job. These are angels in Satan's kingdom, in a total battle against God. "Angel of the Lord" can mean either a good or evil messenger. In Job they are called "sons of God." All creation originates from God and he gave his creation freedom of choice whether to serve good or evil, even to angels.

God tempted Abraham. He tempted David to number Israel and scripture says Satan was actually the one who did this, based on David's failure in the law. "A lying spirit from God" led astray an evil king. This all points to spiritual powers in battle against God's creation. It shows God's true nature: he suffers a committee and devil's advocate to examine him.

In Egypt, God "passed over" Israel to shield them from the destroyer (see also Isaiah 31). Passover means God stood between his people and the destroyer. God was not the killer, but the deliverer.

5. *God's wrath in the Wilderness*

"The law brings wrath". The destroyer in the Wilderness was not God, but the accuser (1 Cor 10:10). Satan stood to accuse God for bringing up an unholy people from Egypt. We see the same when God brought them out of Babylon (Zechariah 3). In the Wilderness God says he will destroy, but this means he will give way to the destroyer. It is actually the accuser who leads into sin and by that "steals, kills and destroys."

The contrast between a God of love who frees his people from bondage and the God of fire on the mountain is stark. He called them to relationship, to be his precious possession and reflect his love in the nations. But like Adam, they too refused to believe in God's love and accept his intimacy. So they also sided with the devil's advocate in their hearts and came under his captivity and thereby needed the law to save them. The law required nationalism, war and death to sustain, but it's a system Israel chose due to unbelief. God said they would be caught through the law in Satan's snare (Deuteronomy 28, Romans 7). The law, nationalism and war failed to deal with sin, even in Israel itself.

When in doubt about the meaning of a passage of scripture as to the nature of God, default to Jesus Christ in the Gospels, who refused to call down fire on sinners, but said "Father forgive them". Do not side with the Pharisees to accuse and destroy.

6. *Ethnic cleansing in Joshua*

That idea is not a true account of Joshua. Joshua attacked the military strongholds. Phrases like, "he put to the sword everything that breathed, man, woman and child", were not literal, but expressions of speech. The text in Joshua itself, as well as other ancient documents, show this. There are good books available that look at this in great detail, for example *Is God a Moral Monster?* by Paul Copan.

Contrary to the vision of a God of wrath, what we see in Joshua is a God who says, "When you enter the land, love the foreigner and stranger, just as I loved you and delivered you from bondage." The purpose of Christ's kingdom is to mould our cultures into his loving Jubilee nature.

God told Israel not to have a king, not to be like the nations around them, not to build fortresses, or amass armaments or horses, and not to hold a standing army, but to love their neighbour, to do justly to their own people and to love their enemies, and God would care for them. The Sermon on the Mount was not new. The empires that David and Solomon built were not God's purpose. Though he gave them his grace and riches, they were still not clothed like the lily of the field.

In Joshua we see the "ban" on all idolatry, but in Jesus we do not see this. Jesus did not drive sinners from the land. He gave his life for his enemies, to change their desires. This troubled the Pharisees and so Jesus called them to show self-giving mercy to God's people. Joshua's "ban" is not our model of God's nature, Jesus is.

7. *The atonement*

A theory of the atonement that became popular in the medieval age reflects more on the nature of human culture than it does on God. This theory stresses that God is like the human king who is personally offended by wrong done to him, and God, like that king, must have payment, reparation, or satisfaction.

This was not the main view of the early church. Even today, it is not the view held by all Christians. The Gospels seem to present a different view of the atonement, where God forgives freely, and is only looking for repentance. Jesus tells us therefore to forgive freely, without satisfaction, for this is what our Father does. Jesus is against satisfaction ("eye for an eye"). In the Prodigal Son, the father forgives and longs for his son's return, without any satisfaction. At other times, Jesus simply says, "Your sins are forgiven..."

In the Gospels, the work of Jesus is seen as a rescue mission from Satan, from sin, from death and from the law. He says, "Shouldn't this woman, bound all these years by Satan, be loosed on the Sabbath?" The Sabbath and Jubilee are a release from Satan's bondage, like the Exodus, release from Pharaoh's captivity. Jesus then describes his atoning death as a "ransom for many".

"For the Son of man came not to be served, but to serve, and to give his life as a ransom for many." This becomes the defining image of

God's nature and our posture as his church and followers.

The early church saw the cross as God "passing over" us: that is, between us and Satan, who was legally correct in demanding God maintain a holy position in his law, but wrong in his motivation. God established and satisfied the conditions of a covenant (bore the wrath for our disobedience) to save us in a just manner, demonstrate his love and cleanse our conscience. He took the accuser's destruction himself. He did no violence and demands no violence. All the violence done was by man, absorbed by God himself in Christ, to save us from sin, death and the law. Christ rose to give us eternal life. As a friend said, "Jesus did not save us from God, but revealed God as saviour."

Even animal sacrifice in the Old Testament was not the will of God. Not many in the Old Testament could see past this cosmic battle between God and sin, to see the true self-giving nature of God. But some prophets did and they proclaimed his real character, just as Jesus showed it.

The cross conclusively proves God's complete rejection of the violence, finger pointing and scapegoating inherent in the human heart and cultures. All these things he bore, but none of them did he demand.

We emulate the cross, not by demanding satisfaction, but by freely forgiving and offering ourselves as servants to our brother and sister, to society and to our enemy. We emulate the cross by restorative, (loving, forgiving) justice, not by demanding punishment and punitive satisfaction. Those who live like God in Christ are the children of God.

When in doubt about our doctrines, look at Jesus and what he taught and did. Whether going back to the Old Testament, or forward to Paul and Revelation, understand what was said through Jesus.

8. *Eternal judgement*

Space does not allow us to look at this fully. We can be assured with Abraham, "Shall not the judge of all the earth do that which is right?" This means right before his accusers, before the conscience of man, and in light of the general grace he has given to the world. God does not act like an unanswerable dictator, even though he has the right and power to do so.

Christians have different views on the nature of eternal judgement, whether in the end it is destruction of the sinner's life, or eternal conscious torment. We need to go by scripture, in its own context, and not by our personal or group convictions. There are many relevant passages from the Old and New Testaments. Many passages use apocalyptic symbols, so in taking a literal stand on all the details we may not be correctly motivated.

This is a serious topic, but we are wrong to use such teachings of eternal conscience torment, which again became prevalent in the medieval age, to paint our picture of who God is, and use that to justify an unloving attitude ourselves towards others.

In obeying Christ, the main lesson we can take from the passages on judgement is that God is judge and this teaches us not to judge, slander or gossip about others, but instead to give ourselves for them in word and deed. When Naaman was healed of leprosy, he asked that the Lord overlook him bowing down in a pagan temple for the sake of his king. He said in his heart he would be bowing to the Lord. God sees our heart, wherever we bow down. Jesus said this type of thing many times to the Jews of his generation. Do not judge, but support others.

God does not ask us to do anything that he does not do himself. He asks us to forgive freely because he forgives freely. He asks us to love the unlovely because he loves the unlovely. He asks us to do what is right in the eyes of all men, because he himself does not act in an unanswerable way to his own creation. If we think God acts in an unaccountable way, then we will do the same to those we consider to be under us.

Our view of God affects how we treat people in our marriages and in our social customs. In many ways these views need to change. We have too often seen him as a feudal hierarchical lord and translated that into our own relationships. God acts in love towards his creation. Be God's children: act like him. That is what he asks.

9. Governments bear the sword to kill

Paul said this about the Roman government in Romans 13. He called them "God's ministers" in the sense that he allows evil governments to curtail other evil people. They were to be respected, like Daniel had respect for Nebuchadnezzar. That does not mean these governments do God's will. Paul was speaking about the believer having respect and honour for governing bodies. Paul was not naïve about the abuse of Rome, and he witnessed to the lordship of Christ against it. Revelation also describes that government as a beast.

The scriptures show that governments are to be renewed and transformed, to rule by justice and compassion, not to exalt themselves over people, but to be humble and serve humanity's wellbeing, just as God does. Governments do not have a licence from God to serve national self-interests, while not caring about, perhaps even contributing to the suffering of others.

We need to take care in how we use scripture to endorse "military solutions." In every place where insurgency has taken root there has been long term regional and global injustice which has prepared the ground. Effective united community orientated policing may be a better response than self-serving strategic alliances. Church community life needs to be a leading witness for regional care, regardless of the population's religious or political affiliations. This heals. "The fruit of justice shall be peace."

Governments typically build empires. God wants his people to model and build community which will renew the world powers. Therefore, to the believer Paul says, put on and be transformed into the image of who Jesus is:

"Do not conform to the pattern of this world, but be transformed by the renewing of your mind. Then you will be able to test and approve what God's will is - his good, pleasing and perfect will... Love must be sincere. Hate what is evil; cling to what is good. Be devoted to one another in love. Honour one another above yourselves. Never be lacking in zeal, but keep your spiritual fervour, serving the Lord. Be joyful in hope, patient in affliction, faithful in prayer. Share with the Lord's people who are in need. Practice hospitality. Bless those who persecute you; bless and do not curse.

Rejoice with those who rejoice; mourn with those who mourn. Live in harmony with one another. Do not be proud, but be willing to associate with people of low position. Do not be conceited. Do not repay anyone evil for evil. Be careful to do what is right in the eyes of everyone. If it is possible, as far as it depends on you, live at peace with everyone. Do not take revenge, my dear friends, but leave room for God's wrath, for it is written: "It is mine to avenge; I will repay," says the Lord. On the contrary: If your enemy is hungry, feed him; if he is thirsty, give him something to drink. In doing this, you will heap burning coals on his head (convict their conscience). Do not be overcome by evil, but overcome evil with good."

In all these areas, a God who is love, who is holy and just, is acting in a sinful world against his enemy Satan, working through his new kingdom to transform our hearts and our nations after his own image and likeness, revealed to us in its fullness without blemish in Jesus Christ. Going through the scripture with a concordance, we see that God abhors violence.

We see God's nature in what he does about his enemies. He serves them, and in doing so declares his will for us to follow. He is transforming us into his image, until we, "beat our spears into instruments of peace", and "the wolf lies down with the lamb." This is the nature and program of his church.

What is Discipleship?

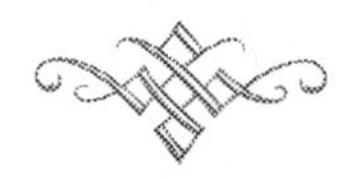

Look at the state the world is in today! How did it get like this? Religion is part of it. Is that why God gave us knowledge of himself, so that we could divide over issues? We have taught the knowledge of God, as though that is what people need, but not discipled and led them by example in the way of God. We havc not donc the things that God does, because we have not known him, known his real nature and what he is really like.

The world needs healing and for that we need radical change. In everything, Jesus taught that the solution started with God's people, with the log in our eye. Change starts in the household of faith. So here are a couple of areas we offer for consideration.

1. *It's what we do, not what we believe*

We have majored on our beliefs, and these have separated us from each other in the church and from others outside the church. This separation is one of our biggest issues today in why the world is in its current state. We build camps and do not love and help our neighbour. Religion becomes that which separates us, but in all

Jesus' teaching it is to be that which drives us to our neighbour, to help and care for their needs, no matter who that neighbour is. What has gone wrong with our hearts? Why have we turned Jesus' teaching and clear life model upside-down?

In the Sermon on the Mount, Jesus did not teach about what we believe, but spoke about what we do. When we go through each section of this sermon it is all about lifestyle. Nowhere in this sermon is there a list of the things to believe. Just think about this. The Sermon on the Mount is Jesus' main message on how to be his disciple. We have thought discipleship is putting people through a class on the doctrines of our faith; no wonder we are in the state we are in today.

Discipleship is how to follow Jesus in our relationships with others, to reconcile, to give our lives in helping to bring healing to our community. Discipleship is our commitment in faith, by his Spirit indwelling us, to love one another and to love our enemy: to care about their personal needs. Love is put above all our personal concerns and needs, as it was in Jesus' own life. This is what he taught us and called us to follow as his disciples.

In the days of Constantine, the first Christian Roman emperor, the posture and flavour of the church in the world changed. Constantine forced uniformity in his kingdom and made the bishops "agree" on doctrine. They drew up the Nicene Creed and attached the anathema: "Cursed is everyone who does not believe" this list of necessary things. They punished "heretics" and put unbelievers to the sword. Augustine, the theologian, actually justified what he termed "persecution" of heretics by joint state-church power. This completely turned Jesus' posture ("my kingdom does not use worldly means") on its head. Churches have stood on Augustine's view, to a greater or lesser extent, until today.

It was in Constantine's time that what it means to be a disciple changed. Rather than laying down our lives for all people, we became separated into political camps based on our doctrines. An unrecognisable Jesus became the figurehead of our own earthly kingdoms.

James addressed this issue. He wrote before Jerusalem fell in AD 70, when the region was in an awful mess, very similar to the way things are in the world today. Division and lack of care for others abounded. James addressed the things that heal. He addressed the issue of real faith, or genuine discipleship, head on.

We can draw up a quick list from James: honour all people with equal respect, whatever their class or background; do not judge and speak ill of others; repent from all forms of violence (greed and immorality); look after the poor; care for all those hurting; put them above our own investments; do not demonstrate our faith by our beliefs, but by our actions towards others.

How can we drive past a hungry person and say we believe the right things? How can we ignore the suffering of refugees, boat people, Muslims, orphans, widows, poor kids, other cultures in our society, economic slaves (often women), or "sinners" just because they are not part of us? When we serve them we are healed. When we search for others we are found. We are healed together. It's when we say we are not sick that we cannot be healed. James is a peacemaking, community restoring letter, given at a very critical time in history; but at the time they did not hear. Will we hear today?

Today, we have a world ravaged by divisions, national interest and violence, which is leaving great numbers of people suffering. The solution is easy, though it means taking up our cross and following Christ. This is the real Breaking News we live out: "So many people are helping others in their daily needs, despite their religious or political affiliation. Instead of arguing, people are caring for each other, and laying aside their differences. Instead of finding fault with our nation and the events that are happening, people are thanking God for their lives and for his goodness. If this keeps up the situation could become very serious, as things in our societies begin to sharply improve."

"I was hungry and you fed me." Christ calls all those suffering his brethren, our neighbour. Putting people's needs above our fundamentalism and reasons for division is the church's true way. We say, "What about our faith, what about what we believe?" This is how we establish our faith, by living and showing it.

Rome's pagan Emperor Julian (fourth century) said: "(The Christian faith) has been specially advanced through the loving service rendered to strangers, and through their care for the burial of the dead. It is a scandal that there is not a single Jew who is a beggar, and that the godless Galileans (that is what he called Christians because they would not worship idols) care not only for their own poor but for ours as well; while those who belong to us look in vain for the help that we should render them."

Christians loved and cared for Jews and pagans, just because they were people. To compete with the Christians Julian embarked on moral reforms in the pagan temples and welfare throughout his empire. These Christians did not protest; they served. When the Romans threw away their unwanted babies to die, the Christians took them in to raise them. When people were dying of plague, the Christians risked their lives to nurse them. On and on the examples go; this is how they changed their world. It is living the creeds, not protesting them.

To Jesus and James, as in Hebrew culture, believing meant doing. "If you were Abraham's seed you would do the works of your father Abraham." When the Gospels speak of believing on Jesus they mean embracing him as Lord, which means becoming his disciple. Believing is not separated from repentance and his new way of life. Faith and works are the same thing, inspired by his Spirit. Not works of religious custom, but the works of our heavenly Father, following his action as seen in Christ.

2. *What do we value?*

In a day and time when there is so much suffering in the world, when communities need healing and care, what are our values? What do we care about? If we go on caring about our own needs only, and not the needs of others, our communities will go into further neglect, division and trouble.

Let us spend less on our buildings and more on caring for the needs of widows, orphans and refugees; single parents; needy children; destitute elderly. Let us not only care for Christians in our community, but also for Muslims and their needs as people. Let us go to the Muslim elders in our community (even in the West) and sit down and talk to them. Find ways of integrating and helping their community. Let us get back to the days when Muslims and Christians showed care to each other in the places they lived. We are to love others whether or not they receive the gospel. This is genuine witness.

It is not evangelism by social care. That does not work. It is care for its own sake. It is just living the Christian life. It is the gospel and the Spirit who changes the heart. We are called to show the change in our heart, as we share his truth in love.

Caring for others should be our number one concern and expenditure in time and funds. This is responsible parenting. We are parents and leaders in our community. Why do we value buildings and personal possessions above people? Because we value personal prestige. It is the buildings and "success" in the world's eyes that give us prestige. People will ask what have we achieved, what do we have to show? Jesus will ask us, what have we valued, and he will answer himself with the evidence of what we have done with our lives in truly caring for others (Matt 25:34-46).

People matter most to God and therefore they must matter most to us. Until we have come to this type of life, our communities will not be healed. When we repent in this matter, all things in this world regarding healing and restoring are possible. "You shall be called repairers of the breach."

So let's not take the higher seats at the meetings, but present ourselves as joyful servants, loving every person around us and seeking their full maturity in love as our main endeavour. If a cyclist arrives at our church he/she is as valuable as any other person and should feel just as comfortable parking their bicycle in the prime parking spot as the pastor does. We need a culture where we love each other and value each other as persons, no matter our class, no matter our gender, no matter our faith, no matter anything. This is what James taught, and this is what is going to heal our land.

It is time to pray and time for radical change from the heart outwards. This is what Jesus spoke on concerning our land, how God's kingdom comes and brings us into his good land. Discipleship is recognizing and loving our brother and sister in Christ, and loving and caring for our enemy. It is putting these matters above our personal prestige. This is what Jesus taught in the Sermon on the Mount. As a friend said, "Salvation is a restoration project, not an evacuation project."

"Enter in at the narrow gate." (Matt 7:13) What is that narrow gate? The previous verse: "Whatever you desire others to do to you, do to them. For this is the law and the prophets." Jesus actually said we are to "work hard" to do this. Again in Luke, "Enter in at the narrow gate... for many shall say Lord, Lord but shall not enter." And in Matt 25, the narrow gate, "Lord, when did we see you hungry and feed you...?" The narrow gate: his fruit. Faith does not replace this, but real faith produces fruit. Sowing the seed of the kingdom: the seed is in the fruit.